Hurricane

by Verna Allette Wilkins
illustrated by Tim Clarey

Tamarind

Tamarind

Published by Tamarind Ltd, 2004
PO Box 52
Northwood
Middx HA6 1UN

Text © Verna Allette Wilkins
Illustrations © Tim Clarey
Edited by Simona Sideri

ISBN 1 870516 66 4

Printed in Singapore

Chapter 1

The harsh clanging of the old, brass bell shook the early afternoon quiet at St Patrick's School. It sparked off a noisy buzz among the two hundred pupils.

"What's going on?"

"What's happening?"

"What's that about?"

"Could be the storm!" Troy said to his classmates. "It was on the news this morning. But my Dad said it was heading somewhere else and…"

"Quiet now," shouted Mr Belgrave, the class teacher, above the din.

There was a short, sharp knock and the classroom door swung open. A prefect rushed in and handed the teacher a slip of paper. He then hurried off in the direction of the next classroom.

The teacher glanced at the paper. "Children," said Mr Belgrave quietly, "collect your belongings and report to the main hall."

By the time Troy's class reached the hall, all the other pupils and their teachers were assembled there. Miss Fergus, the head teacher, stood on the stage and demanded everyone's attention.

"A hurricane is in the area," she said. "It was moving north, but it has turned and we are now lying in its path. We could be in for a direct hit. Sandy Bay has already been devastated. Some people have, regrettably, lost their lives. It's a terrible storm. It's very important that you collect all your belongings and go home. Immediately."

There was great excitement in the assembly hall. None of the pupils could remember having an unexpected half-day off school.

Grandma's horribly scary hurricane stories flashed through Troy's mind. "Stories… that's all they are," he thought. Gran's gory stories, his mother called them. Stories about high winds that ripped off tin roofs and swung them around like samurai swords, cutting off the heads of people running for shelter from the wind and rain. Stories about landslides that swept houses downhill and left them miles away from where they once stood. Forked lightning that slammed into trees and killed everyone standing underneath, sheltering from the rain. With a shudder of rising panic, Troy shut the 'gory stories' out of his mind.

Another thought sprang into his mind. *His little sister…* He needed to find her.

"How can I do anything with a whingeing little sister stuck to my heels?" he asked himself. "I have to take her everywhere. Even if I manage to escape, it's never for long. She could find a needle in a haystack," he muttered, and broke into a jog.

Troy was two years older than Nita and had strict instructions from his parents always to take care of her. She was eight. "I'm old enough to look after her," he thought, "but not old enough to go to the cinema on my own. Not old enough to stay out after dark, or go swimming with the boys. Doesn't make sense… anyway…"

He zig-zagged his way through the crowd of excited children until he found her. "Nita, come on, let's go!" Troy called out to her.

They joined the girls and boys racing down the hill from the huge, old schoolhouse. Some children waited to be collected by their parents. Others headed home on foot. Some clambered onto buses near the large open market. Many of the stallholders had already left. Others were hurriedly packing up.

"Tell you what, Nita," said Troy. "Let's go to Clive's house. He has some brilliant new games and we can play for a while. We can go home later, before the hurricane hits."

"Do you think we should, Troy?" said Nita, hesitating.

"Come on. We have loads of time. Don't worry!" said Troy.

"But, Troy, everyone's rushing home!"

"Come on, grumpy! Clive has a new wheelchair. A really whizzy one. He's been racing it up and down the deck. He wants us to see it. Let's go."

Chapter 2

A minibus came speeding along and Troy waved it down. The door swiftly slid backwards and the conductor jumped out.

"C'mon kids. Get in quick." He helped Nita on and pushed Troy into a few inches of seat near the door, then squashed in beside him. He seemed to fold himself up and then dragged the door shut. Off they raced in the direction of Clive's house.

Above the frisky drumming of calypso music on the driver's tape, the passengers spoke loudly to make themselves heard.

"This one will hit us hard. It could be as bad as Hurricane Bertha. I will never forget that night," said the old man in the front seat, holding his head in his hands. "We lost everything in that storm!"

"I hope it doesn't hit us before tonight or tomorrow," said the driver. "I have to take this bus to the garage and then get all the way home again."

"It might never happen anyway!" said one passenger to no one in particular. "We had two warnings last year. Do you remember? All we had was some crashing loud thunder which made the children hide under the bed and then some high winds that blew the washing off the line!"

"I know some bad things will happen. I can feel it in my bones. It's going to be a terrible one," said one woman clutching a very small child on one knee and a huge shopping bag on the other.

"She's just like Grandma, isn't she?" Troy whispered to Nita, nudging her in the ribs.

Nita didn't even smile. She just chewed the nail on her little finger.

By the time the bus arrived at Clive's house, the wind was blowing stronger and the slender oleander trees were swaying back and forth. Clouds were scooting across the sun and casting long dark shadows on the hills. The women along the road were holding on to their hats.

"Troy," said Nita. "I think we should go back. We should go home."

"Oh no! We're here already. We'll just have a few games. We won't stay long. Come on."

They jumped off the bus and raced down the steep hill to Clive's house. They knocked on the door and waited. Then they knocked again. And again.

Troy ran around to the kitchen door and came racing back to Nita, who was standing on tiptoe, nervously peering through a window. "They're not in. Even the dogs have gone, Nita," he said. "Let's go."

Running back up the hill against the growing wind was difficult.

"I hope a bus comes soon," gasped Nita in a trembly voice.

Cars and trucks drove up and down the road, but only a few buses raced by. None going in their direction. The wind was blowing more briskly by the minute and the tall, thin coconut trees were bending low. When the sun did not reappear from behind a huge, dark, grey cloud, Troy too began to feel nervous.

They stood for nearly twenty minutes waiting for a bus.

"Where do you think Clive and his family have gone?" asked Nita.

"S'pose they went to his Auntie's house in Caribo. Maybe they think that if the storm is bad and the house is damaged, it'll be hard to get him up the hill in his wheelchair."

"Do you think it'll be that bad?" muttered Nita, shuddering.

"Dunno… Hope not… Just want to get home… Where's that bus!!"

None came. They began to walk.

"Should we ask for a lift, Troy?" asked Nita.

"We'd better not. Mum warned me about taking lifts from strangers."

"Oh Troy. It's getting really horrible!" wailed Nita.

"Let's run, then," said Troy.

By then the wind had changed from a frolic to a rushing, wild gallop. One gust pitched into them, pushed them along and they ran and ran.

All along the road, they saw people hurrying home. The windows of a few houses were boarded up.

Chapter 3

Suddenly, Troy stopped. "I know a shortcut through here," he gasped. "We might get a bus at the other end."

Before Nita could argue, a bolt of lightning ripped through the clouds. It felt like a thousand camera flashes going off at once. Nita screamed at the top of her lungs. The shiny surfaces of the broad banana leaves lit up a dark, narrow path, just off the road. A sudden horrendous slam of thunder nearly deafened them.

Troy grabbed Nita's hand and dived down the path. He dragged her along, almost blindly, as the wind whipped twigs against their bodies, stinging their faces. Large leaves slapped their arms.

Suddenly, Troy tripped and pitched forward taking Nita down with him. They both screamed.

He had tripped on a rope stretched tight across the path. A young goat, tied to a tree, had panicked in the fierce weather, and run from one side of the path to the other. The frightened animal had tangled its rope around a large tree stump and now stood, half strangled, bleating feebly.

"It'll die if we don't help, Nita," said Troy scrambling to his feet. He untangled the rope from the broken branches and led the frightened animal back to the tree it was tied to. He patted the poor animal's shivering head.

They carried on nervously along the path and just as Troy was beginning to think that he had taken a wrong turning, he

heard a noise. "A bus. A bus. I can hear a bus. Come on, Nita," he shouted.

They leaped across the huge gutter between the track and the road, in the nick of time, to catch the bus going in the direction of home.

The driver went as fast as he could. He drove against the wind. Branches whipped in front of him. A sudden blast of torrential rain made it almost impossible for his windscreen wipers to work properly and for him to see the crossroads ahead.

He slowed right down. "I'll take the low road by the bay," he said eventually, as the wind lashed the little bus. "The high road is just below Mount Vale and I'm betting that it's already blocked by a landslide. It's a nasty road."

He swung the bus down along Bay Road. They had only driven for about half a mile when the bus swerved madly and jolted to a stop. Everyone pitched forward.

"Lord save us!" shouted one man at the back of the bus. "I'm too young to die!"

"Sorry everybody!" the driver called out. "Don't worry son, wasn't trying to kill you. I thought that tree was going to fall on top of us!"

The tall coconut trees were bending near to breaking point, then flinging themselves upright again after every gust of wind. The driver carried on slowly.

"Will we get home, Troy?" asked Nita.

"Where do you think we're going, silly?" asked Troy, trying not to shiver.

"Listen, son," said the bus conductor, "she has every right to be scared. Storms can kill."

Nita nodded. "See!!" she muttered.

Outside, another fierce gust of wind tore coconuts off trees and sent them bouncing along the road and all around the bus. The driver swerved to avoid them. Nita wept silently while Troy pretended not to notice.

Once they had crept past the line of coconut trees, the driver sped up. The passengers were silent.

They were very close to another row of trees. A blinding flash of forked lightning zig-zagged downwards, right past the windscreen. Even the most ferocious roll of thunder could not silence the splintering, cracking noise. Everyone pitched forward as the bus again jerked to a sudden stop. The grey day had turned completely dark.

"Everybody out!" screamed the driver. "A tree hit us!"

He crawled out of his seat, through the broken window and helped the passengers, one by one, to get out. They fought through the broken glass, leaves and branches of the tree to get to safety.

The driver stood, shaking his head and staring at the caved-in roof of his beloved red bus. The passengers stood and watched. The heavens opened once again and the rain pelted down on them. They were drenched to the skin.

"Are you going towards Mornay?" Troy asked one person.

"Yes. Come with us," she said.

They battled on against the wind and rain.

Chapter 4

It was nearly dark, although it was only half past two in the afternoon. Every few minutes, bolts of forked lightning ripped through the sky and lit up flying plastic bags, twigs and various bits of debris. Thunder roared and the wind became wilder and wilder.

"Troy," wailed Nita. "The rain's got in my bag. My books are all wet and mashed up."

"It's not your fault. Come on. Keep walking." He reached over to touch Nita's bag, slipped and fell on a patch of slimy, mangled bananas. The squashed fruit felt nasty and was all over his shorts and bare legs. "Wait!" he shouted.

"Come on!" yelled the woman they were following. "We've got to keep going because…" A loud clap of thunder cut off the rest of her words and she ran towards a huge rock to hide. They all followed.

Huddled behind the rock was an old man. He was wet and weary.

Troy walked over to him and said, "Mr Prosper?"

"Yes… Oh, Troy!" murmured the old man. "It's a bad one, y'know. As soon as the rain eases up, we should try and get out of here. Stony Hill is right above us and there could be a landslide. It's not safe here."

"Troy. Come here! Who is that?" whispered Nita.

"It's Mr Prosper. Can't you see?" he said quietly. "Y'know,

he lives in the rickety old house on stilts. The house Dad says is a disgrace. Rags for curtains and an old box for a front doorstep… Gran says one day the wind will…"

"Shhh…" whispered Nita, shivering violently. "He might hear you!"

"Yes, OK… He might help us. We'll follow him home," Troy whispered on, so no one would notice how badly his teeth were chattering.

The little group bunched together for half an hour but as soon as the wind calmed down they decided to move on.

"If we take the track that runs along the back of the sugar factory," said Mr Prosper, "I think we can make it home. The track is longer, but because it's in the valley, it's safer. If we can't get home, maybe someone will let us into the factory."

Troy and Nita wished the rest of the group good luck. They set off, with Mr Prosper walking ahead of them, his head bent into the strong wind.

By the time they reached the sugar factory, the storm seemed less fierce. The trio walked on until they arrived at the foot of a steep hill.

"Grab the vines hanging from the trees to steady yourselves and keep moving," called Mr Prosper.

"Help!" wailed Nita. "I've lost a shoe."

"Mr Prosper! Wait!" screamed Troy. He turned and leaned backwards to try and help his sister. As he grabbed the shoe, he slipped, fell and slid sideways into a deep gully.

"Mr Prosper… Nita!" he shouted.

Mr Prosper turned back swiftly, grabbing vines and shrubs as he slithered down. Nita followed. Troy was clinging to a branch, his eyes wide with fear. The soft earth crumbling away beneath his feet.

He was just out of reach.

"Here!" said Nita to Mr Prosper. "Take this." She pulled off her tie and knotted a loop at both ends.

"Clever girl. Here lad! Grab this." Mr Prosper held onto a tree and lowered a loop to Troy, "We've got you!" he cried as Troy grabbed it. "Leave your school bag. It's too far to reach."

Troy clambered up and Nita helped him to his feet. She put on her shoe and they set off again.

Nearby they found a path and after a half hour's walk they saw some houses.

"That's your place over there," said Mr Prosper. "Look. Even your tree-house is still there!"

Mr Prosper ran toward his rickety home on stilts on the side of the hill.

"Where on earth have you two been?" their mother asked, her voice shaky with relief and worry. "Your father left work at the airport and is out there in that terrible, terrible storm searching for you! Where have you been? We called the school. You were sent home ages ago."

Both children stood silent and guilty, grateful for the dim candlelight that scarcely lit up the large room.

"We went to Clive's house," said Troy meekly.

"What! Clive's house? What for?"

Troy looked down at his soggy shoes and Nita stood quietly.

"OK, OK, you two. Just go upstairs and get out of those wet clothes. All I need is for you to go down with double pneumonia. Grandma's made some hot pumpkin soup so hurry up. Go on. And I just hope your father gets back here safely."

They both shot out of the room before their mother could mention their filthy clothes.

"Don't be too hard on them, my dear," said Troy's grandma, coming out of the kitchen carrying a large tureen of piping hot pumpkin soup. "They really don't know what a hurricane can do. They're too young."

"Your gory stories were surely scary enough to make them understand what a killer a hurricane can be," replied Troy's mother.

From his bedroom, Troy heard a loud knocking on the front door. "Nita, Dad's back. We can go downstairs, now."

"It's really serious out there," they heard Dad say. "Thank goodness they're safe."

Chapter 5

Bedtime was early that night. No giggles. No pillow fights. No electricity, so no television.

"Can we have candles so we can read?" asked Nita.

"No you can't!" her father answered, his voice tense with worry. "All we need is one falling over and setting this place alight. We'll go up in smoke in minutes in this wind. Just go to bed."

The children scurried upstairs. The hurricane continued to batter the island.

"Nita!" said Troy, hesitating. "The window's moving!"

"Silly! That's the tree moving, not the window!" said Nita, yawning. They were exhausted and soon fell fast asleep.

A loud, splintering crash woke them. The terrified children leaped out of bed and dashed into the corridor.

The large tree at the front of the house had smashed through the front window. Long branches and broken bits of their tree-house poked into the house and blocked the stairs. The wind whistled in and blew books and ornaments about.

"The storm! It's in here!" yelled Troy, as a bolt of lightning ripped through the house.

In the brief silence between one crash of thunder and another, Troy and Nita shouted, *"Daddddddd! Muuummm!"*

They heard their father's voice struggling against the noise of the storm. "Troy! Nita! Can't get to you! Stairs

blocked!" The children saw that the branches were so dense, their father was too big to get through the gaps.

Troy crouched down onto the floor, shivering. Nita edged her way between the leaves and branches, stepping carefully over the broken glass. " Troy, quick!" she said. "We have to do this. C'mon!" Very gently, she took his arm. She squeezed between the smaller branches and, pulling Troy behind her, edged their way down the trunk.

They jumped to the ground at the front of the house and banged on the door. "Mum! Dad!!"

Both parents grabbed the children and hugged them. "We're in here!" said their father. "The front room isn't safe!"

The back room was full of people. There was a neighbour in every chair. The Watson family, all eight of them, were seated on the floor, lined up against the wall.

Grandma was in charge. "C'mon you two. Sit with me." She settled back into her rocking chair. "This storm will go on all night long… Get comfortable everyone."

Then she began one of her gory stories. "There was a really, terrible storm, thirteen years ago," she said in her gravelly voice. "The winds were so strong grown men were blown off their feet. One woman found a great big boat in her yard… She didn't even live near the sea. A humongous wave just lifted the boat and dumped it there. Then that same wave dragged her neighbour's house back into the sea with the people still in it. All around the village, tin roofs from houses whirled in the air like samurai swords…"

"Oh… the samurai swords are out," joked Troy's mother. "The Titanic is sitting in someone's garden… Oh boy!"

Undaunted, Grandma carried on. "Landslides swept everything down into the valley below, houses, people, animals, trees… There was nowhere to hide…"

"Please Grandma, stop! You're scaring everyone," wailed Troy. Outside, the storm howled on.

"… Well," continued Grandma, "unless you lived in a big, strong, solid house…"

Frantic knocking at the front door interrupted her. Everyone jumped.

Troy's mother rushed to open it, screamed and half shut it again. "It's Mr Prosper. The wind's ripped all his clothes off. Quick! Hand me something to cover him. "

Grandma pulled the tablecloth off the table. "Here! Use this!" she said, and threw it in the direction of the door.

As Troy's mother helped the old man into the room, she said, "Nita! Find one of Dad's shirts. Hurry, Mr Prosper's shivering."

"Are you OK? Not hurt are you?" Grandma asked.

Mr Prosper put one hand to his forehead and the other clutched the tablecloth to stop it from slipping. Both hands were shaky. "I've lost everything. The house is gone. I've nothing left. Nothing."

"Here's some hot pumpkin soup, Mr Prosper," said Grandma and settled down to telling even more gory stories.

After about three hours, the storm grew quieter and some of the younger guests fell asleep.

Chapter 6

Early next morning, Grandma asked for helpers and disappeared into the kitchen to cook for everyone. Outside, it was deathly quiet.

Troy ran to open the front door. He couldn't believe his eyes. He grabbed Nita's hand and they stood stock still on the front steps and stared. It looked as if a giant in a ferociously nasty mood had come out of nowhere, uprooted dozens of trees, snapped off branches, stamped on houses, knocked roofs off, flipped cars over and then just disappeared.

"Where's everything? It looks so different! Troy, this is creepy. I can't even remember what was where," said Nita, shocked at the devastation.

They clambered over the fallen tree. The garden was littered with broken branches, clothes blown off lines from miles away and bits of tin roof. "Oh no! That's where Mr Prosper's house was! Y'know, Dad was always wishing that it would disappear, and now it has…"

"Look, there's Mr Prosper! Shhh…." said Nita.

Mr Prosper was walking towards the space where his house once stood. His frail body was shrouded in an enormous shirt reaching well below his knees. Both hands were out of sight halfway up the sleeves, the ends flapping empty.

"This is weird!" said Troy. "Yesterday, when we left for school, we could only see as far as the top of the road. Now, look! We can see for miles."

There was no birdsong. This was the time for the noisy cockerel to cock… a doodle… doo… and strut across the yard. He was silent and nowhere to be seen. The sun was rising in a clear, cloudless sky and not even a breeze brushed their cheeks.

There was a noise from the side of the house as their father clambered over the fallen tree to reach the front door.

"I hope it's only that window I have to repair. Don't know what damage is underneath the branches. The roof is fine. You kids ok?" he asked.

"Fine, Dad. Can we do anything?"

"I'll manage, and your mother and grandmother are sorting out that lot in there. Old Prosper is already asking your grandmother to alter some of my trousers to fit him…"

"Dad!" said Nita, "We'd still be out there, lost somewhere, if he hadn't helped us. He brought us home last night!"

"Oh! I didn't know. I'll shut up now and go thank him…"

"No problem sir!" chuckled Mr Prosper. "I suppose it's all right for me to stay in your house, now? I'll just go back indoors and find somewhere comfortable to sleep!" He ducked back into the house.

Through a side window, the children could see their mother bow her head and shake it from side to side.

"Troy! Nita! Come with me," said Dad. "We can't do anymore here. I have to check out the airport to see what damage there is to the planes."

Parts of the main road were blocked by fallen trees. Abandoned cars, trucks, buses and many of the small houses near the road had been flattened in the storm. People were searching through the rubble collecting what they could find of their belongings. The big houses were standing, but some had lost their roofs. No cars passed, even the emergency vehicles were stranded until the roads could be cleared.

"Look what I've found!" shouted Nita. She picked up a large road sign. "It says Belmont."

"How far is that, Dad?" asked Nita.

"About two miles! See how strong the wind was!"

"Did it fly through the air, all the way here?" asked Nita.

"Like a samurai sword!" giggled Troy.

Four people came towards them carrying a fifth person on a stretcher made from a door. The injured man looked very poorly with a blood-soaked bandage around his head.

"I hope they make it to the hospital. There'll be no transport anywhere," said Troy's father. "Do you need help?" he asked then.

"Not far to go now, thanks!" gasped one of the men. They looked exhausted.

Then another group walked past heading for the hospital too. They took turns carrying a sick child.

"It'll take us years to recover from this one!" muttered their father. His face was gloomy. His jaw set tight.

Chapter 7

They worked their way slowly along the road to the airport where they met Clive's father.

"Everything OK at your place?" Dad asked him.

"Don't know yet," Clive's father replied. "I didn't manage to get home yesterday. Stayed in that building over there all night!" He pointed to a small concrete shelter half hidden among the trees. "Clive and his mother escaped just before lunch and went to Caribo. Our area is known for landslides. This storm is really bad news for us. We had just decided to move because it is so difficult to get Clive up and down that steep hill in the wheelchair. Now, if there's been a landslide, we've lost everything!"

"No. Maybe your place is OK. Let's hope for the best," said Troy's father.

"Hmmmm…!" muttered Troy. "Hope they don't move far! Clive's got some seriously good games!"

All the buildings at the airport were still standing. One large passenger aircraft sat on one side of the airport undamaged. However, the smaller planes had suffered badly. One was completely upturned, wheels skyward, and a mangled wing crunched sideways.

"Was Hurricane Bertha as bad as this, Dad?" asked Troy.

"Bertha was worse than this," said his dad. "This island of ours really suffered. We lost all that year's crops of bananas

and sugar cane. We still haven't recovered from the loss of the nutmeg trees. They take years to grow. Those were hard times."

"By the way, kids, I've heard your school's roof has blown off," said Clive's father. "It'll take a long while to repair. Terrible, don't you think?"

"Terrible," muttered Troy and Nita together. They exchanged a wink and a smile.

"Well, there's nothing we can do today, because the repair teams won't be able to get here," said Dad. "Come on kids, let's go home."

"How was it?" asked Grandma as soon as they stepped into the house.

"Very bad, Grandma," said Nita. "Exactly like your gory stories."

"See," said Grandma. "What did I tell you? But, remember that after all the drama of a storm comes this lovely calm. And eventually, everything grows and blooms again."

OTHER TAMARIND TITLES